A Plant Called Spot

Nancy J. Peteraf

A PLANT CALLED
SPOT

Illustrated by Lillian Hoban

A Doubleday Book for Young Readers

A Doubleday Book for Young Readers
Published by
Delacorte Press
Bantam Doubleday Dell Publishing Group, Inc.
1540 Broadway
New York, New York 10036

Library of Congress Cataloging in Publication Data
Peteraf, Nancy J.
A plant called Spot / Nancy J. Peteraf : illustrated by Lillian Hoban.
p.   cm.
Summary: Teddy learns how to care for animal pets after his mother buys him a pet plant.
ISBN 0-385-30885-X
[1. Pets—Fiction.   2. Plants—Fiction.]   I. Hoban, Lillian, ill.   II. Title.
PZ7.P441543P1   1994
[E]—dc20   92-27474   CIP   AC

Manufactured in Italy
April 1994
10   9   8   7   6   5   4   3   2   1
Nil

In loving memory of my mother,
Wanda Romańska Peteraf

"I'd like a pet," Teddy said to his mother.
"Can I have a dog?"

"We already have a dog," replied his mother.

"But Sam doesn't like me," said Teddy.
"He likes Daddy best."

"Your daddy takes Sam
for walks every day,
and plays fetch with him.

Perhaps if you didn't pull his tail,
Sam would like you better."

"Can I have a cat?" Teddy asked.
"We already have a cat,"
said his mother.

"But Kitty doesn't like me," Teddy said.
"She likes Tommy best."

"Your brother Tommy
lets Kitty sit on his lap,
and gives her
fresh milk to drink.

Perhaps if you didn't chase her away
from her favorite place by the fire,
Kitty would like you, too."

"Can I have a rabbit?"
Teddy asked his mother.
    "We already have a rabbit,"
his mother replied.

"But Fluffy only likes Janie.
He doesn't like me," said Teddy.

"Your sister Janie feeds Fluffy fresh carrots and lettuce, and changes his cage every day.

Maybe if you didn't yank his ears,
Fluffy would like you better."

"I still want a pet of my very own," Teddy said.

The next day Teddy's mother came home from the store
and handed a bag to Teddy. "Here is your very
own pet," she said.

Teddy opened the bag and looked in it. "But
that's a plant!" he cried.

"It's your pet plant," said his mother. "You must
water it, and see that it gets plenty of sunshine,
and take care of it. It's your very own plant."

Teddy sighed, and took the plant up to his room. "You don't look like a very good pet to me," he said to the plant. "But since you're all my mother will let me have, I think I'll name you Spot."

Teddy looked after Spot,
and watered him
carefully.
He kept him
on a sunny windowsill
in his room.
And sometimes
he sat by Spot
and read to him.
And Spot grew.

Kitty came in and poked her paw at the plant.
"No, no, Kitty! You mustn't play with Spot,"
yelled Teddy. "If you promise not to hurt Spot,
I won't chase you anymore, and
I'll give you fresh milk to drink."

Sam came running into Teddy's room, wagging his tail and sniffing the plant.

"No, no, Sam!" Teddy cried. "You'll knock Spot over with your tail. If you promise to be careful, I won't pull your tail anymore, and I'll play fetch with you."

Fluffy hopped into Teddy's room, and started to nibble Spot's leaves.

"No, no, Fluffy! You mustn't eat Spot!" cried Teddy. "If you promise to leave him alone, I'll feed you fresh carrots every day, and I'll never, ever yank your ears."

Every day from then on,
Teddy played with Sam the dog,
and petted Kitty the cat,

and fed fresh carrots
to Fluffy the rabbit.

And he kept a close watch on all of them to make sure that they didn't hurt Spot the plant. And Spot grew.

Teddy sat in his room and read to Spot. And Sam and Kitty and Fluffy came in to listen, too. And Spot grew.

And then one day…

Spot BLOOMED!